I Took the Moon for a Walk

Written by **Carolyn Curtis**

Illustrated by **Alison Jay**

Barefoot Books
step inside a story

I took the Moon for a walk last night.

It followed behind like a still summer kite,

Though there wasn't a string or a tail in sight,

when I took the Moon for a walk.

I carried my own light just in case

the Moon got scared and hid its face.

But it peeked through clouds
that were fragile as lace,
when I took the Moon for
a walk.

I warned the Moon to rise a bit higher,

so it wouldn't get hooked on a church's tall spire,

And the dogs of the town made a train-whistle choir,

when I took the Moon for a walk.

We tiptoed through grass where the night crawlers creep

when the rust-bellied robins have all gone to sleep,

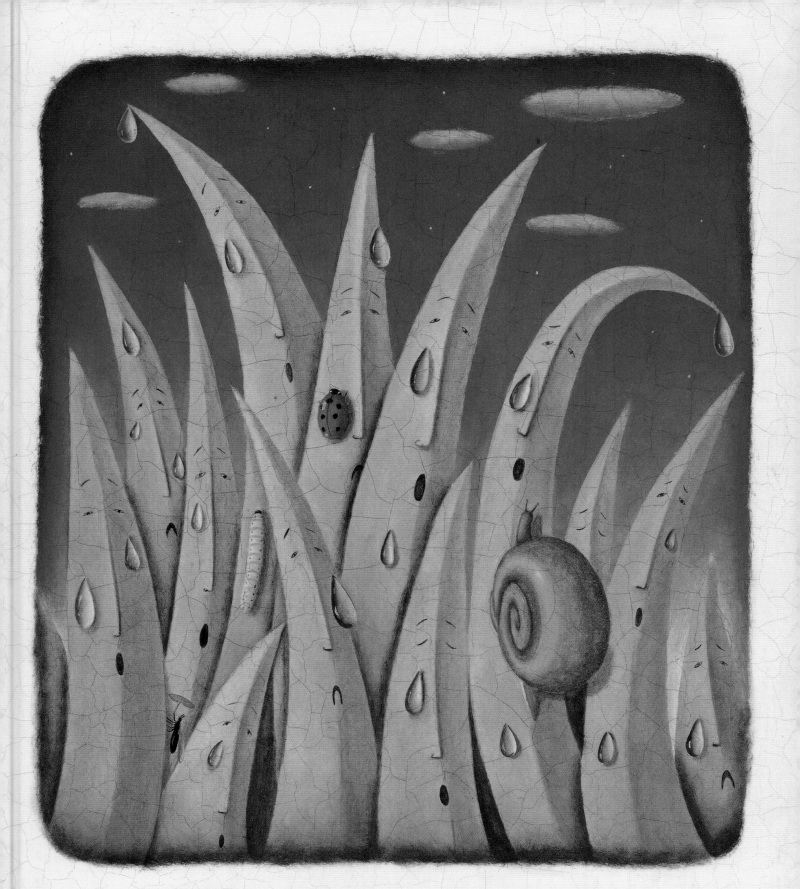

And the Moon called the dew so the grass seemed to weep,
when I took the Moon for a walk.

We raced for the swings,
    where I kicked my feet high
and imagined the Moon
    had just asked me to fly,

Hand holding hand through the starry night sky,

when I took the Moon for a walk.

We danced 'cross the bridge where the smooth waters flow.

The Moon was above and the Moon was below,

And bright in between them
            I echoed their glow,
when I took the Moon for
                   a walk.

Then as we turned back, the Moon kept me in sight.

It followed me home and stayed there all night,

And thanked me by sharing its sweet sleepy light,

when I took the Moon for a walk.

The Mysterious Moon

What do you see when you look at the moon? Children who live in Europe and the United States imagine that they see a man when they look at the moon. Children in Japan and India see a rabbit, and children in Australia see a kitten. But all children, no matter where they live, look up in wonder at the same moon.

The moon is primarily made of rock with a small iron core. It creates no light of its own, but reflects sunlight.

The shape of the moon seems to change during the month because the sunlight strikes the moon at different angles as it travels through space. These shapes are called phases. Here are some of the phases of the moon:

New Moon   *Crescent Moon*   *Half Moon*   *Gibbous Moon*   *Full Moon*

When the moon is getting larger in the sky, we say that it is waxing. When it is getting smaller, we say that it is waning.

For people all over the world, the moon has always been an important way to measure time. Although the solar calendar has become the standard international way of doing this, many people still use lunar, or moon, calendars.

The moon can be a friend to farmers and gardeners — those who follow tradition know that the best time to sow seeds and transplant young shoots is when the moon is waxing.

Moon festivals are celebrated in many societies. The Chinese Moon Festival is held during the harvest moon — the full moon that rises in mid-autumn.

Many Celtic and Native American festivals are also held at the time of the harvest moon, when the people give thanks for the harvest and for all living things on Earth.

The World at Night

If you took the moon for a walk where you live, what would you show it? What would you hear, and what would you see?

Wherever you are, you would probably see some nocturnal creatures — mammals, birds and insects that usually sleep during the day and come out to hunt and eat at night. They are especially adapted to life under the moon and stars:

Cats have eyes that see very well in the dark.

Rabbits have large ears that capture sound across long distances.

Bats use sounds and echoes to help them fly safely and find food.

Fireflies light up at night so that they can find each other.

Owls have necks that can turn right around and huge, flat eyes that enable them to see creatures that are far away.

Some flowers are nocturnal too. They bloom and release their fragrance after dark.

And although you are asleep during the night, your mind is not! During the day your waking, or conscious, mind is active, but when you sleep your dreaming, or unconscious, mind is busy. So, the world at night is not as quiet as it seems!

For my nephew Christopher, who first walked the Moon
and my mother Estella, who held his hand
For my father Harold, the Star we steer by
and Lucan, my Sun
and, of course, for Emilie, for Everything — C. C.

The author extends heartfelt thanks to WarmLines Parent Resources, Jane Yolen, the Jeff Kelly and Newton Library Critique Groups,
Alison Keehn, and the Society of Children's Book Writers and Illustrators for generous support in the form of a Barbara Karlin Grant.

For Mark, happy moon walking, love from Alison.

Barefoot Books
294 Banbury Road
Oxford, OX2 7ED

Barefoot Books
2067 Massachusetts Ave
Cambridge, MA 02140

Text copyright © 2004 by Carolyn Curtis
Illustrations copyright © 2004 by Alison Jay
The moral rights of Carolyn Curtis and Alison Jay have been asserted

First published in Great Britain by Barefoot Books, Ltd
and in the United States of America by Barefoot Books, Inc in 2004
This paperback edition first printed in 2012
All rights reserved

This book was typeset in 22pt Legacy Serif Book and Fontesque Bold
The illustrations were prepared in alkyd oil paint on paper with a crackling varnish

Reproduction by B&P International, Hong Kong
Printed in China on 100% acid-free paper

ISBN 978-1-84148-803-5

British Cataloguing-in-Publication Data: a catalogue
record for this book is available from the British Library

Library of Congress Cataloging-in-Publication Data
is available under LCCN 2003019087

5 7 9 8 6 4